THE MARZIPAN MOON

THE MARZIPAN MOON

Nancy Willard

Illustrated by

Marcia Sewall

HARCOURT
NEW YORK • BRACE • LONDON
JOVANOVICH

Requests for permission to make copies of
any part of the work should be mailed to:
Permissions, Harcourt Brace Jovanovich, Inc.,
757 Third Avenue, New York, New York 10017.

Printed in the United States of America

LIBRARY OF CONGRESS CATALOGING IN PUBLICATION DATA
Willard, Nancy.
The marzipan moon.
SUMMARY: The almonds in an old, mended, but magic crock
produce a delicious, nourishing marzipan moon nightly
for a poor parish priest until a visiting bishop decides
the miraculous almonds need a more fitting home.
[1. Magic—Fiction] I. Sewall, Marcia. II. Title.
PZ7.W6553Mar   [Fic]   80-24221
ISBN 0-15-252962-4   ISBN 0-15-252963-2 (pbk.)
BCDE   First edition   BCDE (PBK.)

Happy birthday, John!

NOW THEN, the story begins.

There was once an old priest who had in his care a church so poor that even the mice stayed away. On Sundays a handful of old women came to the services. They didn't look happy. Why should they? The church was so cold that they had to wear their coats and boots and mufflers, and still their feet froze and their hands turned numb. There was a big furnace but no money for oil, and plenty of fireplaces in the parish house but no money for firewood.

The priest's birthday fell in February, and every year the women left their gifts for him in his study. Some baked cakes, some made marzipan, some knitted mufflers. The cakes and marzipan went quickly enough, but a man can wear only one muffler at a time, and mufflers rarely wear out.

Now there was in that parish a woman so poor that she had hardly a penny for herself, let alone for the priest. But as the priest's birthday drew near, she happened to spy on her way to church a clay crock that someone had thrown into the garbage.

"Cleaned up," she said to herself, "that would make a handsome present."

And she knelt down and fished it out. Then she saw why it had been thrown away. The crock was cracked quite in two.

Nevertheless, she took it home and glued the two halves together. When the priest's birthday arrived, she left her gift in his study with the others.

In the evening, when the priest opened his presents, he discovered that everyone had knitted him mufflers. No one had thought to bake him a cake, or make him marzipan, which he dearly loved, for he only got it on his birthday and sometimes at Christmas. The crock perplexed him. He peered hopefully into it and was much disappointed to find it held nothing but the moonlight pouring through the window.

"Oh," said the priest with a sigh, and he laid his hand on the crock as he spoke. "How I wish I might find a marzipan moon on my kitchen table every morning!"

He carried the crock to his kitchen, put it in the cupboard, and went to bed hungry.

What was his surprise the next morning to find on his table a marzipan moon of the finest quality. He could not imagine how it had got there, for no one kept the key to his house except himself. But he ate it with great relish and thanked God for remembering him.

The following morning the priest could scarcely believe his eyes when he found on his table a second marzipan moon, exactly like the first.

"Someone," he said to himself, "is playing a joke on me."

As he spoke, his glance fell on the crock. Then he remembered how he had rested his hand upon it when he wished for a marzipan moon every morning.

"Is it a magic crock, then? Let's see what else it can do," he said. Laying his hand on it, he wished for enough firewood and oil to keep the church warm all winter.

"Leave the wood in the boxes by the fireplaces, Lord," he added, "so I needn't carry it from the woodpile in cold weather."

The next morning he hurried around to all the fireplaces, but the boxes were empty, and the inside of the church was as cold as the outside. The marzipan moon, however, lay on his table as usual.

"So it grants only one wish," said the priest sadly. "If I had known that, I would have wished for something more sensible."

Still, he had a marzipan moon for breakfast every morning, so he was better off than before. That winter he lived on tea and marzipan, a diet likely to kill you if you stick to it long enough. But the old priest never felt better in his life. The marzipan seemed to give him strength as well as sweetness. And he never forgot to thank God for re-membering him.

When the bishop made his annual visit in the spring, the priest invited him to his house after the service and served him a cup of tea and a marzipan moon. It was all he had to offer him.

After the first bite, the bishop closed his eyes.

"Never," said the bishop, opening them again, "have I tasted finer marzipan. Where did you buy it?"

"That marzipan," said the priest, "was made by no human hands."

And then he told the bishop about the wonderful crock and how the Lord left him a marzipan moon every morning. The bishop listened with great interest and declared,

"What makes you think the gift is from God? You must stay awake tonight and watch. It might be from the devil."

Such an idea had never occurred to the priest, and he was very much frightened. The bishop, however, offered to stand watch with him. And that night they set the crock on the table and hid themselves in the broom closet, being careful to leave the door open a crack.

For a long time they heard nothing but the ticking of the clock. On the last stroke of midnight, there came a humming and a rustling, and out of the crock leaped two almonds, which rolled about on the table and split open.

Wonder of wonders! Out stepped two re-
markable creatures. Their bodies were old
flour sacks, their legs old mufflers, their arms

sticks of firewood, and they had the heads of the queer animals carved long ago on the choir stalls in the dark corners of the nave.

They were as tall as the bishop in his miter, and they fluttered their great wings as they stood before the priest's oven and sang,

"God bless the living,
God bless the dead,
God bless the flour,
God bless the bread."

Then they opened the oven and took out of its cold darkness a marzipan moon, which they left on the table, and they stepped back into their almond shells, and the shells closed over them, and the almonds leaped back into the crock again.

The bishop and the priest burst out of the closet.

"It is a miracle!" exclaimed the bishop. "They are spirits, angels, I know not what!"

"It is a miracle," said the priest, "and very good marzipan."

They sat down at the table, and the bishop ate the marzipan moon, quite forgetting to offer any to the priest.

"This old crock is hardly a fitting home for a miracle," said the bishop. "It's cracked down the middle. It should have been thrown away long ago."

"Hardly a fitting home," agreed the priest, who wondered how he had never noticed the miraculous almonds that lay in the crock.

"I shall order a new one," said the bishop, "made of gold. And it will stand in the cathedral where everyone can see it. You shall come with me and assist me at services. I will send someone to fill your post here."

And I shall have a marzipan moon every morning, he thought, but of course he did not say this to the priest.

The priest was sad to leave his old parish. "At least I will be warm and have enough to eat," he told himself.

And so the bishop ordered a more fitting home for the miracle, and you never saw a more splendid one: a casket of gold, trimmed with silver wrought into arches, under which stood Matthew and Mark and Luke and John, and all the best people in heaven. The pearls around the rim were plump as peas, the rubies big as acorns.

And when it was finished, the bishop sent his car for the priest, who climbed in, clutching the clay crock, and rode twenty-five miles from his church to the steps of the cathedral. The bishop came out to meet him.

A choir sang and the organ played while the bishop moved the two almonds from the old clay crock to the casket of gold, which was placed on the main altar. No spirits could have asked for a better housewarming.

The clay crock was tossed into the garbage.

The next morning the bishop hurried to the altar to fetch the marzipan moon. But he found none there, nor in his kitchen, nor in the casket itself, which held nothing but the two almonds.

"I will stay awake tonight and watch what happens," said the bishop.

"And I will stay with you," said the priest.

So the bishop and the priest sat in the darkest corner of the choir stall and watched the casket, expecting at any moment to see the almonds leap out into the candlelight.

But nothing happened.

The marzipan moon did not appear that morning, nor the next morning, nor the morning after that.

"The Lord giveth and the Lord taketh away," said the bishop.

Because he had paid a good deal for the casket, he put it in a glass case by the front door of the cathedral, with a little sign describing the miracle, and if no one has taken it, I suppose it's there yet.

But the clay crock, now, that's the one you want to get hold of. And if you do, remember the priest's story.

Wish for something sensible.